RIDE THE RAINBOW

To our David and Alejandra
*Your beautiful marriage
is a multicultural embrace*

Story and Songs
by Karen Seader

Illustrations by Valerie Lynn

Song Illustrations by Laurie Getlan

D1531180

In Your Heart Lives a Rainbow, LLC

Published by **In Your Heart Lives a Rainbow, LLC**

Text Copyright ©2007 by Karen Seader
Illustration Copyright ©2007 by Valerie Lynn

First Edition 2014

All Rights Reserved
No part of this publication may be reproduced or transmitted in any form or by any
means, electronic or mechanical, including photocopying, recording, any information
storage or retrieval system, without the prior written permission from the publisher.

ISBN: 978-0-9857824-2-9

Library of Congress Catalog Card Number: 2013917964

Manufactured by Color House Graphics, Inc., Grand Rapids, MI, USA Job# 42411, March 2014

Music and Lyrics Copyright ©2006 by Karen Seader
Musical Arrangements by Larry Sacchetillo

Book 1 includes CD of 11 songs for the first three books of the series.
Song tracks correspond to the illustrated song pages in each book.
The songs can also be downloaded from our website:
InYourHeartLivesaRainbow.com

Karen Seader - author, singer, and songwriter, along with her sister Valerie Lynn - illustrator, co-created the **In Your Heart Lives a Rainbow**® book series with original songs. Combining fantasy and reality, this dynamic, innovative series focuses on character building and positive life skills to make a significant difference in children's lives.

We thank our sister Laurie Getlan, for contributing her artistic talents to create the beautiful song illustrations in this book, and for helping to edit the book series.

"Our goal is to reach and empower children, families, and educators, to be a motivating and nurturing force that **brings out the best in children** and **brings Love and Unity into the world**."

BOOK 3 - *Ride the Rainbow*
Hailey, Logan, and their friends from around the world go on a flight of fantasy on an ever changing rainbow. They learn that even though the world is very large, we are really just one big family.
The story focuses on giving, sharing, and spreading happiness to one another.

Karen Seader is the co-creator and the author, singer/songwriter of the **In Your Heart Lives a Rainbow**® book series.

She embodies **The Lady of the Rainbow**®, the magical character who inspires and motivates the children. Karen has used the medium of entertainment for more than 20 years to work with over 50,000 children in interactive shows performed at schools, libraries, organizations, camps, parties, and community events. "I truly love connecting with children as **The Lady of the Rainbow**® and creating joyous and meaningful events! I see how receptive they are to the positive, uplifting concepts that are offered in the stories and songs."

Valerie Lynn is the co-creator and illustrator of the **In Your Heart Lives a Rainbow**® book series.

She designed the costume for the **The Lady of the Rainbow**® live show, as well as created the trademarked character. Valerie is a professional fine artist, exhibiting throughout the Northeast. She is a graduate of Parsons School of Design and created her own unique line of fashion artwear, which sold nationally and internationally in fine department stores and boutiques around the world.

Logan heard the mailbox click. "I hope there's a postcard from Grandma and Grandpa for my collection!" Spotting something colorful peeking out of the letters, Logan got excited!

He ran to his room shouting, "Hailey, come and see the postcard from Grandma and Grandpa. It's got a train on it!"

"Show me and I'll read it to you." Hailey said.

Dear Hailey and Logan,

We rode this special train & slept on it too!

Africa is AMAZING!!

We went on Safari...

Saw elephants with gigantic ears & giraffes as tall as trees.

Love,
Grandma and Grandpa

XOX

Hailey and Logan
44 Mart
Northp

R2 South Africa

R10 South Africa

"I'm putting the train next to my Chinese dragon postcard!
Are there real dragons in China?" asked Logan.

"No," answered Hailey, "but there are real kangaroos in Australia.
Look at this funny bird from South America."

"What are these buildings?" asked Logan.

Hailey pointed, "That's Big Ben, the Eiffel Tower and the Coliseum...they're in Europe."

"I like this one," smiled Hailey. "It's from India just like my favorite doll from my collection."

As she took the doll off the shelf... the doorbell rang.

"Sophie and Zabi are here," Mommy called.
"Just in time for a special treat!"

"That's a pretty doll!" exclaimed Sophie.
"Can I play with it?" she asked, grabbing
it out of Hailey's hands.

"Uh oh!" screamed Sophie, seeing the doll fly through
the air and land in the chocolate cream pie.

"I'm sorry," said Sophie.
"I don't want to play with you!" Hailey said angrily.
She started to cry and ran into her bedroom.

She cried herself to sleep and dreamt she was washing her doll.

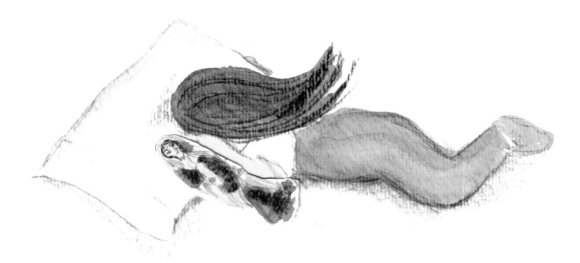

As she squeezed the soap bottle, tiny bubbles floated into the air.

One bubble grew larger and larger with colors swirling inside.

Looking closely, Hailey saw a big word appear... FORGIVE.
To her surprise, JILLY the RAINBOW FAIRY was sitting
right on top of the bubble!

Jilly explained, "When you forgive, you forget something bad
happened and you GIVE someone another chance."

Suddenly, Jilly was inside the bubble. She invited Hailey to come for a ride. Hailey said "Wow!! Can Logan come too? And Zabi....... and Sophie?" "Of course!" giggled Jilly.

Instantly, everyone was inside the bubble laughing with excitement!! The bubble floated right out of the kitchen window into the sky.

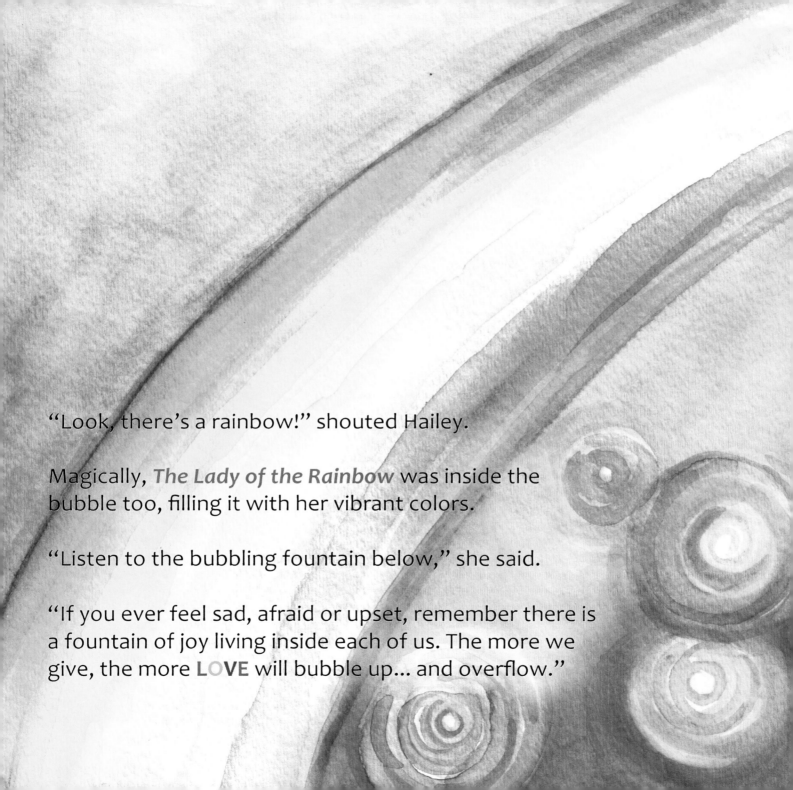

"Look, there's a rainbow!" shouted Hailey.

Magically, *The Lady of the Rainbow* was inside the bubble too, filling it with her vibrant colors.

"Listen to the bubbling fountain below," she said.

"If you ever feel sad, afraid or upset, remember there is a fountain of joy living inside each of us. The more we give, the more LOVE will bubble up... and overflow."

Fountain of Joy

I can feel it in my heart
The boundless stream
of which I'm part
Bubbling over and over again

It's deep inside of me
Ever new and flowing free
It's wonderful just to be

CHORUS
The more we give
The more we live
As love grows
The more it flows

It's deep inside of me
Ever new and flowing free
A Fountain of Joy
For you and me

I can feel it in my heart
The endless stream
of which I'm part
A Fountain of Life and of Love

Amazing to see
The water's flowing buoyantly
It's a Fountain of Joy
For you and me

CHORUS

I can feel it in my heart
The special world
of which I'm part
We're members of one grand family

Every moment we're free
To choose the way to be
To make a better place for you and me

CHORUS

The sparkling fountain turned into a river and then an ocean.

The children looked down and saw the
7 continents of the world.

The Lady of the Rainbow explained, "These are the
different lands where people live. Even though the
world is very large, we are really just one big family."

The next thing they knew, the bubble had burst!

Be kind means to be gentle and friendly

Care is to show concern and be helpful

Give means to offer someone a something special

Now they were dancing around a beautiful maypole, holding long rainbow colored ribbons. Three new children from other lands had joined them... Ming, Isabella and Ajit.

Share is to experience means to be grateful

Appreciate something with others

Respect is to treat others

Enjoy means to delight in things you do

with courtesy

"Look, there are 7 of us!" exclaimed Zabi.
Ming shouted, "Let's move the ribbons and make them ripple
like a fountain!"

The Lady of the Rainbow explained,

"You can't see **LOVE**, but you can feel it. It's an invisible bond between people.
If you could see love, it would look like a rainbow and feel like silk."

"Hold onto the rainbow and follow me!

I'll teach you a song
in all different languages," she said.

The children felt like they were on a train!

ALL HEARTS UNITED

We're All Connected To Each Other
We Live On Earth Under The Sky Above
It's A Joy To Share With One Another
All Hearts United In A Silken Bond Of Love

English   We're all connected to each other

Spanish   Vivimos unidos debajo del mismo cielo
Veeveemos ooneedos dayvaho del meesmo see-ello

French   C'est une joie de partager ensemble
Say tune jooah de partajay ensemble

Hindi   प्यार के रेशम डोर से सब दिल एक होये
Pyar kay rayshem doorsay subdil ake hooay

Swahili
Tuko zote pamoja
Tooko zotay pamojah

Russian
Мы жсивём на земле под одним небом
Mwee jivium na zimleah pod adneem niabum

Chinese
大家一起来分享快乐
Dahja eechee-lye fensheean kwa-le

Italian
Tutti i cuari uniti in un legame di amore
Toutee kwaree ooneetee in oon laygamay dee amoray

Hebrew
כֻּלָם קְשׁוּרִים בְּיַחַד
Kulam kshoreem bayachad

Arabic
تَعِيشُ فِي عَالَم تَحْتَ سَمَاء وَاحِدَة
Nyeesho fee alam tah tah samaah waheeda

German
Es ist eine Freude alles miteinander zu teilen
Es eest eyenay Froyder ahless mitie-nandare tzu tie-len

All hearts united in a silken bond of love

In fact, the rainbow did change into a train... a **UNITY TRAIN**!!
It was so much fun winding around mountains and valleys!

As the train chugged up the highest mountain, the children held
their breaths... and went right off the cliff into the sky!!

To their amazement, the train turned into a magnificent bird made of dazzling **RAINBOW** colors!

They flew above the treetops and
heard little birds singing.

"One of the trees is waving to us!" Ajit exclaimed.
"That's **FATHER TREE**," shouted Logan.

The children waved back and heard **FATHER TREE**
call out, "Always fly high and reach to the sky!"

On Wings of Love

We can be free
Light as can be
Feel the magic in the air

There's so many people in the world
We see them wherever we go
Everyone's looking for happiness
Let's all RIDE THE RAINBOW

Colors swirl by
As we fly high
High above
On Wings of Love

CHORUS
On Wings of Love
On Wings of Love
We feel like we are flying

CHORUS

If you feel low
RIDE THE RAINBOW
Let the colors lead your way

We're flying high
Up to the sky
There's laughter and lots of smiling

Reach to the sky
Keep flying high
High above
On Wings of Love

BRIGHTLY COLOR EVERY DAY

All good things you do and say
Throughout your lives come what may
Remember that's your way

To **Brightly Color** every day   chorus

Let the laughter in your heart be heard
Let your joy resound
Bring happiness to everyone
Spread it all around

Find the **RAINBOW** in your heart
Find the Colors of Love
Let them ripple and flow
And soar high above

Repeat chorus

The Lady of the Rainbow
made an arc of shimmering colors.

"Remember to always brightly color every day
with the **Rainbow** that lives in your heart."

Acknowledgments

My heartfelt thank you to…

My son and daughter-in-law David and Alejandra, for your enormous help in creating the files for the books and songs as well as your wonderful design input.

The love and support from both of you and Joe, my life partner, have been so meaningful and encouraging to me.

My nieces and nephews, Gillian, Hailey, Joshua, Isaac, and Logan, for being my inspiration in creating memorable characters for the books.

My brother-in-law, Michael Getlan, for your untiring motivation to have the books published. You and Laurie have been instrumental in "getting the message out!"

My sister-in-law, Ellen Seader, reading specialist, and her mother, Erna Chaut, former Dean of the School of Education, Adelphi University. Your assistance with editing have been invaluable. The love and encouragement from you, my niece Jamie Lippiner, and sister-in-laws Joan Seader and Diane Seader, have been a tremendous help to me.

My friends and family, for your enthusiasm, suggestions, and contributions. Sally Smollar and Peggy Gorman-children's librarians, Robert Boyar- marketing consultant, Stephanie Goldreyer and Sondra Levine- editing, Cumi Villagran- for converting the files to PowerPoint and to Joanne Schadler- graphic designer, for creating this page.

My graphic designers at Venture Promotions - Dice Garcia and Yelena Mudretsova, as well as at Searles Graphics - Rob Seifert and Nicole Jakob. You have done an exceptional job preparing the files for print. I truly appreciate your patience and expertise.

My book manufacturer, Color House Graphics, the outstanding company I have chosen. I want to especially thank Sandy Gould for making the experience so pleasant.

My talented musician, Larry Sachetillo, for your musical arrangements and instrumentation that have enlivened the songs with your wonderful spirit.

My Aunt Gloria Stroock, actress, and Uncle Leonard Stern, writer, producer, publisher, for your guidance and for sharing with us your seasoned wisdom and expertise.

I am forever grateful to my sisters, Valerie and Laurie, for working with me as a team to create the first 3 books of our series. It will be a joy to continue working together to complete our goal…
the **In Your Heart Lives a Rainbow** series of 7 books.